For Quinlynn, Keegan,
and Audrey Jo
—H. S.

To my three sons, Carter, Benton, and Sawyer,
and of course, to my long-necked,
spotted (freckled), beautiful wife, Stephanie
—C. R.

First published in the United States of America in August 2016
by Bloomsbury Children's Books
www.bloomsbury.com

Bloomsbury is a registered trademark of Bloomsbury Publishing Plc

For information about permission to reproduce selections from this book, write to
Permissions, Bloomsbury Children's Books, 1385 Broadway, New York, New York 10018
Bloomsbury books may be purchased for business or promotional use. For information on bulk purchases
please contact Macmillan Corporate and Premium Sales Department at specialmarkets@macmillan.com

Library of Congress Cataloging-in-Publication Data
Names: Schulz, Heidi. | Robertson, Chris, illustrator.
Title: Giraffes ruin everything / by Heidi Schulz ; illustrated by Chris Robertson.
Description: New York : Bloomsbury, 2016. | Summary: It seems that giraffes will misbehave whether
attending a birthday party, going to the movies, playing in the park, or just about anything else.
Identifiers: LCCN 2015036433
ISBN 978-1-61963-475-6 (hardcover) • ISBN 978-1-68119-082-2 (e-book) • ISBN 978-1-68119-083-9 (e-PDF)
Subjects: | CYAC: Giraffe—Fiction. | Behavior—Fiction. |Friendship—Fiction. | Humorous stories. | BISAC: JUVENILE FICTION/Animals/Giraffes.
JUVENILE FICTION/Humorous Stories. | JUVENILE FICTION/Social Issues/Friendship.
Classification: LCC PZ7.S3912 Gir 2016 | DDC [E]—dc23
LC record available at http://lccn.loc.gov/2015036433

Art created with good old-fashioned pencil, paper, and imagination, then scanned and completed in
Storyboard Pro by Toon Boom
Typeset in Archer
Book design by Colleen Andrews
Printed in China by Leo Paper Products, Heshan, Guangdong
1 3 5 7 9 10 8 6 4 2

All papers used by Bloomsbury Publishing, Inc., are natural, recyclable products
made from wood grown in well-managed forests. The manufacturing processes
conform to the environmental regulations of the country of origin.

Giraffes Ruin Everything

Heidi Schulz

illustrated by
Chris Robertson

BLOOMSBURY

NEW YORK LONDON OXFORD NEW DELHI SYDNEY

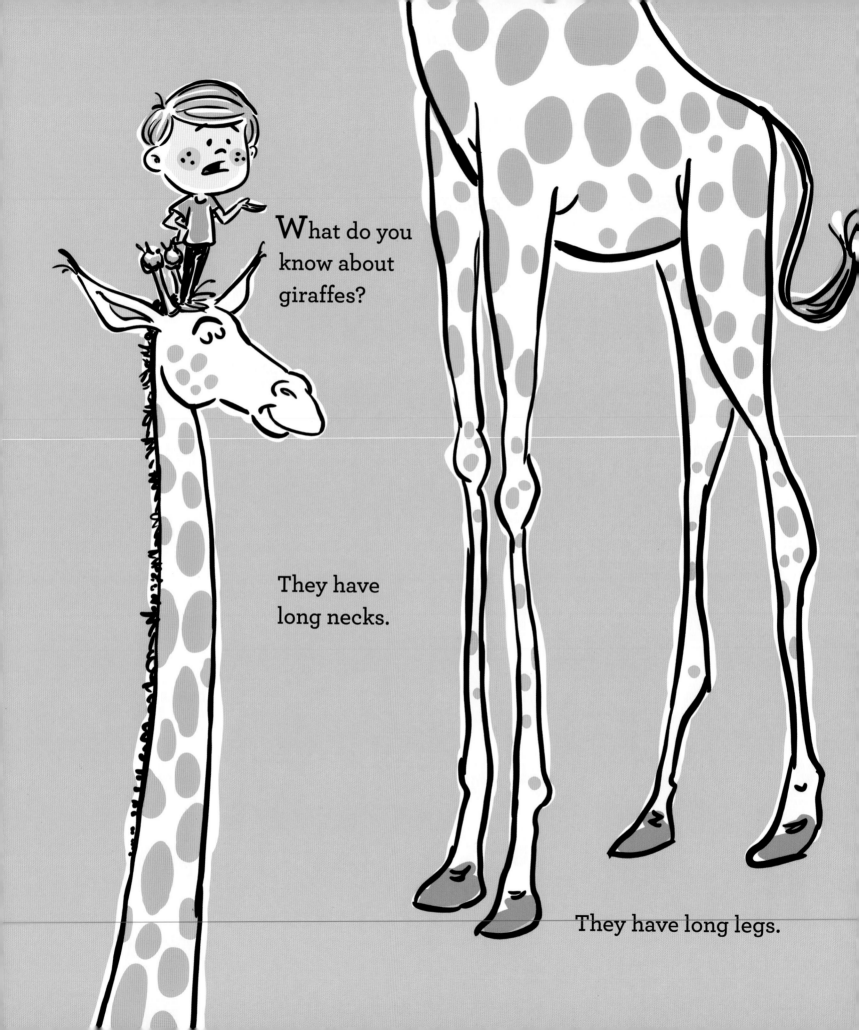

What do you know about giraffes?

They have long necks.

They have long legs.

They are quiet
and gentle and
so very tall.

Did I mention
their long necks?

But that is not all.

There is one more thing you should know about giraffes.

Are you ready?

Giraffes ruin everything.

Happy Birth

If you have a birthday party,
do not invite a giraffe.

He will never say "Would you mind?"
or "If you please."

Instead he will reach his long, long neck
down the table, stick out his tongue, and
slurp up whatever he likes.

And when a glass of punch gets knocked over, staining your favorite T-shirt, the giraffe will not even apologize.

Giraffes ruin everything.

If you wish to go to the movies,
do not invite a giraffe.

He will sit tall in the center seat of the very front row.

His long, long neck will block the screen, so no one can see what is happening.

EXIT

And if you can't tell whether
aliens are landing or a puppy
is stuck in a deep, dark well . . .
the giraffe will pretend not
to notice your frustration.

Giraffes ruin everything.

If you wish to spend an afternoon at the park, do not invite a giraffe.

That is, if you would like
a turn on the slide.

For a giraffe has such
a long, long neck that
when his feet reach
the bottom, his head
is still at the top.

And after you have waited and waited for his turn to come to an end, only to give up and decide to try the swings . . . you will find his legs have already beaten you there.

Giraffes ruin everything.

But that's not even the worst thing about giraffes.

A giraffe will eat the ice cream right
off your cone from half a block away.

A giraffe will win at hide-and-seek.
Even if you are not playing.

A giraffe will peek
into your No Giraffes
Allowed clubhouse,
high up in your
backyard tree,

and steal your
rope ladder right
out from under
your nose.

GIRAFFES RUIN EVERYTHING.

If someone needs help getting
his new kite off the ground,
do not invite a giraffe.

That's a task you'd best undertake yourself.

You could certainly fly it
higher than any old giraffe,
if you tried hard enough.

You know what?
Everyone has bad days
from time to time.

Maybe giraffes are not so terrible after all.

If you happen to find yourself entertaining one, I'm sure—with a little effort—you'll find the right thing to do together.

Just don't invite an elephant.

Elephants ruin everything.